PIGS

A Note from
Robert Munsch

A long, long, LONG time ago when I was in first grade, my class had 60 kids in it!

The teacher didn't read any books and neither did the kids. It was not fun.

Well, here is a book that is fun to read for both you and your grown-ups.

READERS RULE!

High-Frequency Words

Practice reading these high-frequency words in the story:

any open think ran

Meet the Characters

Get to know the characters from the story by looking at the pictures and names below:

Megan

Megan's Father

Teacher

Bus Driver

What do you know?

This story is all about pigs. What do you already know about pigs? Do you think they are smart animals? Do they normally live alone or in groups? Do you think it would be easy to take care of a group of pigs?

Action Words

Verbs are words that describe an action like reading, walking, smiling, or swimming. Take a look at the words below and decide if they are action words:

scream   happy   run   blue

How many action words can you find in the story?

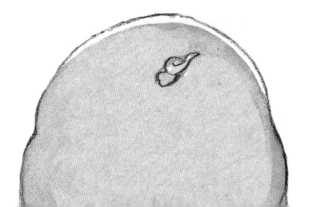

Phonics

There is a **P** sound at the beginning of the word **pigs**.

Can you make a **P** sound?

Pay close attention to the shape of your mouth as you make the sound. It might be helpful to make this sound while you look in a mirror to see the shape your mouth makes.

Try these different activities to help practice the letter **P** sound.

1. Take a close look around you and try to find three objects that start with the same sound.

2. Think of three other words that also start with the same sound. As an extra challenge, can you think of any words that end with a **P** sound?

3. A simple word that has the **p** sound at the beginning is the word **pit**. As you read this word, pay attention to the two other letter sounds in the word.

4. When two words rhyme, they have the same sounds at the end of the word. Take a look at the pictures below and point to any of the words that rhyme with **pit**.

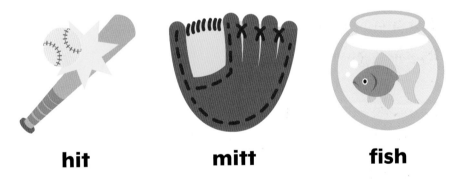

hit　　　　**mitt**　　　　**fish**

5. While you read, look out for other **P** sounds at the beginning of a word throughout the story. You can see the sound easily because it will be written in a different color.

PIGS

Story by **Robert Munsch**
Art by **Michael Martchenko**

annick
press
toronto • berkeley

To Meghan Celhoffer
Holland Centre, Ontario

Megan's father said,

"Megan, please feed the pigs,

but don't open the gate.

Pigs are smarter than you think."

"I will not open the gate.

No, no, no, no, no,"

said Megan.

Megan looked at the pigs and said, "These are the dumbest-looking animals I have ever seen."

She opened the gate a little.

The pigs didn't do anything.

Megan yelled,

"HEY, YOU DUMB PIGS!"

The pigs jumped up—

wap, wap, wap!—

and ran out the gate.

"Uh-oh," she said.

Inside the house, Megan heard,

"OINK, OINK, OINK."

"Get these pigs out of here!"
yelled her father.

Megan yelled,

"HEY, YOU DUMB PIGS!"

The pigs jumped up—

wap, wap, wap!—

and ran out the door.

When Megan got to school,

she heard, "OINK, OINK, OINK."

There were pigs everywhere.

"Get these pigs out of here!"

 yelled the principal.

 Megan yelled,

"HEY, YOU DUMB PIGS!"

The pigs jumped up—

wap, wap, wap!—

and ran out the door.

"That's it! I finally got rid of

all the pigs!" Megan said.

But when she got to

her classroom she heard,

"OINK, OINK, OINK."

Inside her desk was

a new baby pig.

"Get that dumb pig out of here,"

said the teacher.

21

"Dumb? Who ever said

pigs were dumb?

Pigs are smart," said Megan.

"I am going to keep

this one for a pet."

At the end of the day when the

school bus came, Megan heard,

"OINK, OINK, OINK."

"That doesn't sound like

the bus driver," Megan said.

Inside the bus, she saw

pigs everywhere.

A pig shut the door

and drove down the road.

It took Megan all the way home,

and right into the pigpen.

"The pigs are all back in their pen.

They came back by themselves,"

she told her mom and dad.

"Pigs are smarter than you think."

Megan never let out

any more animals.

At least not any more pigs.

Retell Activity

Look closely at each picture and describe what is happening in your own words giving as much detail as possible.

Getting Ready for Reading Tips

- Pick a time during the day when you are most excited to read. This could be when you wake up, after a meal, or right before bedtime.

- Create a special space in your home for reading with some blankets and pillows. The inside of a closet, under a table, or under a bed can make the perfect cozy spot.

- Before you start reading, do a quick look at all the pictures and suggest what the story might be about.

- Can you find the part of the story that repeats?

- Can you add actions like claps, stomps, or jumps to match what is being said to make the words come alive?

- Try to use silly voices for the different characters in the story. Think about changing the volume (e.g., loud, soft), the speed you use to say the words (e.g., fast, super slowly), and how you say the words (e.g., like an animal, like a superhero, like someone older or younger).

- What makes this story silly or funny?

- What part(s) of the story would never happen in real life?

Collect them all!

Adapted from the originals for beginner readers and packed with **Classic Munsch** fun!

Munsch Early Readers — READING LEVEL 3

ANGELA'S AIRPLANE

Story by **Robert Munsch**
Art by **Michael Martchenko**

Munsch Early Readers — READING LEVEL 3

THE FIRE STATION

Story by **Robert Munsch**
Art by **Michael Martchenko**

Munsch Early Readers — READING LEVEL 3

MUD PUDDLE

Story by **Robert Munsch**
Art by **Dušan Petričic**

Munsch Early Readers — READING LEVEL 3

MURMEL, MURMEL, MURMEL

Story by **Robert Munsch**
Art by **Michael Martchenko**

Munsch Early Readers — READING LEVEL 3

THOMAS' SNOWSUIT

Story by **Robert Munsch**
Art by **Michael Martchenko**

All **Munsch Early Readers** are level 3, perfect for emergent readers ready for reading by themselves—because

READERS RULE!

Robert Munsch, author of such classics as *The Paper Bag Princess* and *Mortimer,* is one of North America's bestselling authors of children's books. His books have sold over 80 million copies worldwide. Born in Pennsylvania, he now lives in Ontario.

Michael Martchenko is the award-winning illustrator of the Classic Munsch series and many other beloved children's books. He was born north of Paris, France, and moved to Canada when he was seven.

Designed by Paul Covello

Thank you to Abby Smart, B.Ed., B.A. (Honors), for her work on the educational exercises and for her expert review.

Annick Press Ltd.

We acknowledge the support of the Canada Council for the Arts and the Ontario Arts Council, and the participation of the Government of Canada/la participation du gouvernement du Canada for our publishing activities.

ONTARIO ARTS COUNCIL
CONSEIL DES ARTS DE L'ONTARIO
an Ontario government agency
un organisme du gouvernement de l'Ontario

Library and Archives Canada Cataloguing in Publication

Title: Pigs / story by Robert Munsch ; art by Michael Martchenko.
Names: Munsch, Robert N., 1945- author. | Martchenko, Michael, illustrator.
Identifiers: Canadiana (print) 20210360674 | Canadiana (ebook) 20210360682 | ISBN 9781773216539 (hardcover) | ISBN 9781773216430 (softcover) | ISBN 9781773216669 (HTML)
Subjects: LCSH: Readers (Primary) | LCGFT: Readers (Publications)
Classification: LCC PE1119.2 .M865 2022 | DDC j428.6/2—dc23

Published in the U.S.A. by Annick Press (U.S.) Ltd.
Distributed in Canada by University of Toronto Press.
Distributed in the U.S.A. by Publishers Group West.

Printed in China

annickpress.com
robertmunsch.com

Also available as an e-book. Please visit annickpress.com/ebooks for more details.